I LIKE A SUMMER DAY, IT MAKES ME JUMP AND PLAY,

A SUNNY DAY IS A HAPPY DAY, IT MAKES ME SING THIS WAY!

Cricket and Sparrow

Four Stories by
Edward Bartholic

With Pictures by
Laura Rader

Collins

Library of Congress Cataloging in Publication Data
Bartholic, E L   Cricket and sparrow.

SUMMARY: In four encounters Cricket and Sparrow meet, pretend, visit, and picnic.
[1. Crickets—Fiction. 2. Sparrows—Fiction] I. Rader, Laura.   II. Title.
PZ7.B281277Cr   [E]   78-13141
ISBN 0-529-05512-0   ISBN 0-529-05513-9 lib. bdg.
U.K. ISBN 0-00-183758-3

Published in the United States of America by William Collins Publishers, Inc., New York and Cleveland, and simultaneously in Great Britain by William Collins Sons & Company, Ltd., London, Glasgow and Sydney.

For Veronica and David

Contents

ricket was playing in a big meadow. It was a warm, sunny summer day and he was quite happy. In fact, he was so happy that he hopped and jumped all over the meadow. As he hopped and jumped and played, he sang a summer song.

> *I like a summer day.*
> *It makes me jump and play.*
> *A sunny day is a happy day.*
> *It makes me sing this way.*

Suddenly a big shadow darkened the sky. Cricket looked up and saw a bird standing between him and the sun. "Who are you?" Cricket asked.

"I am Sparrow," the bird answered.

"You are covering up the sun. What do you want?" demanded Cricket.

"You," said Sparrow. "I am going to eat you."

"Why do you want to eat me?" asked Cricket.

"Because you are a cricket," Sparrow replied.

"Do birds eat crickets?" Cricket asked.

"Of course, you silly cricket. Everybody knows that."

"I don't know that," said Cricket. Then Cricket questioned Sparrow further. "Can crickets eat birds?"

"You are the silliest cricket. Of course crickets can't eat birds. Crickets are too little," said Sparrow.

Cricket pondered Sparrow's answer and then said, "I have another question. If I were bigger than a bird, could I eat you?"

Sparrow thought and thought. Finally he answered, "I guess so."

"Well, if I *were* bigger than a bird, I *wouldn't* eat you," said Cricket.

"You wouldn't?" asked Sparrow.

"No, I would *not*," Cricket said emphatically.

Sparrow furrowed his brow. "Why wouldn't you?"

"Because I would want you to be my friend," said Cricket.

"Some places I cannot reach with my beak. Some places I cannot reach with my feet. Some places I cannot reach with my beak *or* my feet. My back is one of those places."

Before Sparrow knew what had happened, Cricket crawled under Sparrow. He began to scratch Sparrow with his hind legs. He scratched so hard feathers flew all over. Feathers flew everywhere.

Sparrow said over and over again, "Oh, that feels good! Oh, that feels good!"

Cricket scratched so hard that soon he was very tired. He lay on the ground gasping for air.

"Are you all right?" cried Sparrow. Finally Cricket sat up. "Yes, but that scratching is hard work."

"I know," said Sparrow, "but you sure are a good scratcher."

"I have a good idea," said Cricket. "If you don't eat me, then you are my friend. If I scratch your back, then I am your friend. That way we can be friends to each other."

Sparrow did not have to think this time. He said, "Yes, Cricket, we can be very good friends. Can you teach me that song you were singing?"

Sparrow knocked on Cricket's door. Cricket didn't answer. Sparrow knocked again. He called, "Cricket, Cricket, it's me, Sparrow." Still Cricket did not answer. Sparrow opened the door and peeked in the house. It was very dark, so Sparrow switched on the light. He looked all around, but Cricket was nowhere to be found. Sparrow went outside. He sat down on the porch steps to think.

Snail was sitting on a rock beside the porch. He saw Sparrow thinking and asked, "What are you thinking about, Sparrow?"

"I am thinking about Cricket. He's not at home, and I don't know where to find him," said Sparrow.

"He went out very early this morning," said Snail.

"Do you know where he was going?" asked Sparrow.

"No, I don't know," answered Snail.

"Thank you," said Sparrow. Sparrow began to look all over the meadow. He looked in the sweet grass. He looked under leaves and on top of logs. He looked under rocks by the creek bank. He looked everywhere. Cricket was nowhere to be found.

Then Sparrow saw Bee sitting on a clover flower. "Good morning, Bee," said Sparrow. Have you seen Cricket? I am looking for him, but I don't know where to find him."

"I saw him very early this morning," answered Bee. "He was by the big oak tree in the middle of the meadow."

"Do you know where he was going?" asked Sparrow.

"No, I don't know where he was going," replied Bee.

"Thank you anyway," sighed Sparrow. Sparrow wondered and wondered, Where could Cricket have been going?

Sparrow decided to fly to the big oak tree in the middle of the meadow and talk to Owl. Owl lived in the big oak tree, and perhaps he knew where Cricket was going. When Sparrow got to the big oak tree, he knocked on Owl's door. After a while, Owl opened the door. He had been asleep and was very grumpy.

"What do you want, Sparrow?" yawned Owl.

"I am sorry to wake you," said Sparrow. "I am looking for Cricket."

"Is that all," answered Owl. "He went past here very early this morning. I know it was early because I hadn't gone to sleep yet."

"Do you know where he was going?" asked Sparrow.

"He was going to the top of the mountain," replied Owl.

"To the top of the mountain!" cried Sparrow.

"Yes," Owl said. "He was going to gather cotton from the clouds."

"Clouds are not made of cotton," said Sparrow.

"You know that. I know that. But Cricket doesn't know that!" exclaimed Owl.

"Thank you, Owl. Thank you very much," said Sparrow.

Sparrow flew as fast as he could towards the mountain. Before he got to the top, he saw Cricket hopping back down the mountain.

"Cricket, I am sure glad to see you," called Sparrow.

Cricket was very sad. "I went to gather cotton from the clouds," Cricket said. "Do you know clouds are not made of cotton?"

"I know," said Sparrow. But he did not like to see his friend so sad, so he said, "I have an idea, Cricket. Clouds are so white and soft and fluffy, let's *pretend* they are made of cotton."

"Is it all right to pretend?" asked Cricket.

"It's all right to pretend if we don't try to fool anyone," said Sparrow.

ne fine morning Cricket decided to visit Sparrow. Cricket had never been to Sparrow's house, so it would be a nice surprise. The only trouble was, Cricket didn't know exactly where Sparrow lived. Well, no bother, Cricket knew Sparrow lived somewhere in the big woods at the end of the meadow. He would just go to the end of the meadow, then ask for directions.

When he got to the end of the meadow, Cricket came to a small dirt road that wasn't used any more. Toad was sitting right in the middle of the road.

"Hello, Toad," said Cricket. "I am going to visit Sparrow. Can you tell me where to find his house?"

"Yes, Cricket," answered Toad. "Sparrow lives in a thicket in the big woods, but I never saw a *cricket* in a thicket." Toad laughed and laughed.

"I don't think that is funny," said Cricket. "I never saw a toad in the road, either."

"Well, you see one now," replied Toad.

Cricket made a chirping noise, then hopped across the dirt road into the big woods. After going a short way, he saw a mouse sitting beside his house. "Hello, Mouse. I am Cricket. I am going to visit Sparrow. Can you tell me where to find his house?"

"Yes, Cricket," said Mouse. "Sparrow lives in a thicket here in the big woods, but I never saw a *cricket* in a thicket." And Mouse also laughed and laughed.

Cricket became angry. "Well, I never saw a mouse in a house," shouted Cricket.

Mouse ran inside his house and poked his head out of the window. "Well, you see one now," he said.

Cricket paid no attention to Mouse and continued on his way. He tried and tried, but he couldn't find Sparrow's house. Cricket looked up at the sky. He hoped to see Sparrow flying around. All he saw was a fly. He decided to ask one more time. "Hello, Fly. I am going to visit Sparrow. Can you tell me where to find his house?"

Fly pointed just ahead. "Sparrow lives right there in that thicket, but I never saw a *cricket* in a thicket." Fly beat his wings with glee.

Cricket stamped one of his hind legs. "Well I never saw a fly in the sky."

"You see one now," said Fly. And he flew all around Cricket's head.

Suddenly Cricket heard a voice. "Cricket, Cricket, what are you doing here?"

Cricket turned to see Sparrow flying towards him. "I came for a visit," answered Cricket, "a surprise visit."

"It is a nice surprise," said Sparrow, "but why do you look so unhappy?"

Cricket replied, "You live in a thicket, and nobody ever saw a cricket in a thicket. Everybody thinks it's funny."

"Is *that* all," said Sparrow. "Hop on my back, and we will fly to the thicket. The whole world will see a cricket in a thicket."

Cricket hopped onto Sparrow's back and off they flew.

45

The Picnic

ricket and Sparrow sat on Cricket's front
porch. They were waiting for their friends.
They were all going on a wonderful picnic together. Each friend was bringing something
good to eat.

"Do you have the mustard, onions, and pickles?" asked Sparrow.

"Yes, they are in my cupboard. I will get
them after our friends arrive," said Cricket.

Rabbit was the first friend to arrive.

"Did you bring the ham and lettuce?" asked Sparrow.

Rabbit did not look very happy. He said, "My friends, I have done a bad thing. I brought the ham, but I ate the lettuce."

Sparrow said, "Don't feel bad, friend Rabbit. Cricket has mustard, onions, and pickles."

"That's right," said Cricket.

"Hello, friend Squirrel," said Mouse.

"Hello to all my friends. I brought the salad," said Squirrel.

"I thought you were bringing salad AND nuts," cried Cricket.

"I ate the nuts. That's why I am so fat," Squirrel said.

Mouse did not mind that Squirrel had eaten the nuts. He said, "Rabbit ate the lettuce, you ate the nuts, and I ate the cheese."

"Cricket has mustard, onions, and pickles. They will do nicely," said Sparrow.

"And Bee is bringing a cake and some honey. I know he will not eat the honey," Cricket said.

Just then, Bee buzzed onto the porch. "Good morning. I know I'm late," said Bee. "I brought the cake, but I was so busy I didn't make the honey."

Cricket just shook his head. He said, "It is time to go on our picnic. I will get the mustard, onions, and pickles." Cricket went into the house. Then all the friends heard Cricket's voice crying: "Oh, my goodness! Oh, my goodness!"

All the friends said together, "What is wrong? What is wrong?"

Cricket ran out of the house. He shouted, "I forgot to buy the mustard, onions, and pickles."

"Oh, Cricket, how awful," they all said. "What shall we do now?"

Suddenly it started to rain. "Did anyone bring a drink?" asked Bee.

"I did. Water!" said Sparrow.

All the friends laughed and laughed—all but Cricket. He felt sad because he thought he had spoiled the picnic. Sparrow noticed that Cricket was not laughing.

"Look, everybody," he called. "We have ham and bread for sandwiches, and we have salad and cake. We have everything we need for our picnic except music. Cricket, will you sing us a song?"

"Oh, yes, sing us a song, please, Cricket," said the others.

"I'd be happy to," said Cricket. And he was.

So they all sat down on the porch—all except Rabbit and Squirrel, who were too big—and they all had a wonderful picnic.